That's Mine, Horace

Holly Keller

GREENWILLOW BOOKS · *An Imprint of HarperCollinsPublishers*

FOR SUSAN AND AVA, ALWAYS

Watercolor paints and a black pen
were used for the full-color art.
The text type is Korinna.

That's Mine, Horace
Copyright © 2000 by Holly Keller
Printed in Hong Kong by South China Printing Company (1988) Ltd.
All rights reserved.
http://www.harperchildrens.com

Library of Congress Cataloging-in-Publication Data

Keller, Holly.
That's mine, Horace / by Holly Keller.
p.   cm.
"Greenwillow Books."
Summary: Horace loves the little yellow truck
that he finds in the schoolyard, but he has a
problem when a classmate tries to claim it.
ISBN 0-688-17159-1 (trade).
ISBN 0-688-17160-5 (lib. bdg.)
[1. Animals—Fiction.   2. Honesty—Fiction.
3. Conduct of life—Fiction.   4. Schools—Fiction.]
I. Title.   PZ7.K28132Th   2000
[E]—dc21   99-19867   CIP

1 2 3 4 5 6 7 8 9 10   First Edition

One sunny morning when the air was filled with the perfume of clover, Horace found a little truck in the schoolyard. It had two tiny doors that opened and closed, shiny red seats, and black rubber wheels that spun without making a sound.

Horace thought it was the best truck he had ever seen.

Mrs. Pepper rang the bell for everyone to come inside.

Horace waited, but nobody came for the truck.

He opened the doors and snapped them shut.

He spun the wheels.

Mrs. Pepper rang the bell again.

Horace looked around.

Nobody was coming, and nobody was watching.

He stuffed the truck into his pocket and ran back to class.

Horace thought about the truck all morning.

It felt heavy in his pocket. He wanted to take it out,

but he didn't dare.

During spelling Mrs. Pepper asked him to spell "tree."

"T-r-u-c-k," he said loudly, and everybody laughed.

By snack time Horace couldn't stand it any more.

He had to roll the truck on the floor just once.

"Hey, that's mine!" Walter shouted when he saw it.

"Horace took my truck."

Horace couldn't believe it. His heart started to pound, and the fur on the back of his neck stood straight up. He put the truck back into his pocket and quickly went to get a cookie.

"Is that Walter's truck?" Mrs. Pepper asked

when she poured Horace's juice.

Horace shook his head.

"No," he said, "it's mine."

Mrs. Pepper patted the top of Horace's head.

"I know you would never tell a fib, Horace,"

she said.

When it was time to go home, Horace didn't wait to say

good-bye to Mrs. Pepper. He didn't want to see her.

He grabbed his lunch box and ran straight home.

He hid the truck under his pillow and left it there until bedtime.

"What a nice truck," Mama said when she tucked him in.

"Where did you get it?"

"Walter gave it to me," Horace said.

"To keep?" Mama asked.

Horace nodded. "His grandpa sent him a new one."

Mama patted the top of Horace's head.

"I know you would never take anything

that didn't belong to you," she said.

Horace turned over and shut his eyes before Mama

could give him his kiss.

Horace woke up in the middle of the night.

It was very dark in his room, and his bed looked

like a big orange truck.

Horace thought it was taking him back to school.

"No," he said out loud. "I don't want to go."

He turned on his light and pulled his blanket up

over his eyes, but he couldn't fall asleep.

In the morning it was raining, and Horace was very tired.

His head hurt, and he had a stomach ache.

Mama called Doctor Singe.

The doctor looked in Horace's ears and listened to his chest.

"I'm sure he'll be fine in a few days," she told Mama.

Horace didn't think so.

"You can stay in bed and play with your truck, Horace,"

the doctor said. "Is it new?"

Horace didn't answer.

Mrs. Pepper called the next day.
She said that Melanie was going to deliver
some get-well letters from the class
on her way home from school.

"Is that all she said?" Horace asked.

"No," said Mama. "She said she thought
you would feel better soon."

The sign on the door reads:

purple bumps
throwing up
and fever
STAY OUT
or you will
catch it !

Horace put a stay-out sign on his door.

But Melanie said she was coming in anyway

because she'd already had all that.

Melanie dumped a big pile of letters onto Horace's bed.

There was a drawing from Alice and a riddle from Fred,

but they didn't make Horace feel better.

There was a letter from Walter, too.

Horace took the paper out of the envelope very slowly.

dear Horace,
I hope you get well soon
and come back to school.
Your friend,
Walter

P.S. it's o.k. for you to keep the
truck until you're all better.
Then you have to give
it back.

The next morning

Horace announced that he felt fine

and he was ready to go back to school.

Mama went into the kitchen to make his lunch,

and Horace looked at the truck.

He opened the doors and snapped them shut.

He spun the wheels.

It really was the best truck he had ever seen.

He put it in his pocket.

"Let's welcome Horace back to school,"

said Mrs. Pepper after she rang the bell.

At recess Horace climbed to the top

of the slide when Walter was at the bottom.

"Here it comes!" Horace shouted, and

he let the truck roll all the way down.

Then he went sliding down after it.

"Come on," said Walter. "Let's play with it in the sandbox."

Walter built a road, and Horace dug a tunnel.

When Mrs. Pepper rang the bell, Walter took the truck.

Then he and Horace ran back to school together.